CW00853976

MY DOG CAN DO THAT

WRITTEN & ILLUSTRATED BY
SANDRA HARMON

Sandy's
Shelf Books

Omaha, Nebraska

Thank you...

To my sister Barbara, my brother Howard, and my uncle Denzel, remembering all the dog adventures we had growing up (so many dogs I could not include them all).

This book also includes family pets of my sister Meadow, and the dogs from my son Brian's home, and the home of my daughter Melinda.

Dogs can be loyal friends, protectors, clowns and occasionally very big nuisances, but we still love them.

Text and illustrations © 2020 Sandra Harmon. All Rights Reserved. No part of this publication may be reproduced, stored in a retrieval system, or transmitted in any form or by any means—electronic, mechanical, photocopy, recording, or any other—except for brief quotations in printed reviews, without the prior permission from the publisher.

Published by Sandy's Shelf Books
www.SandysShelf.com
SandysShelf@conciergemarketing.com

Hardcover: 978-0-9980387-6-6
Kindle: 978-0-9980387-7-3

Library of Congress Cataloging Number: 2019911390
Cataloging in Publication Data on file with publisher.

Production and design by Concierge Marketing Publishing Services.
Printed in the United States of America.

10 9 8 7 6 5 4 3 2 1

"I love my dog," Curt told Elly as they petted Wookie, the St. Bernard.

"He's so smart and he can do anything," he added.

"Last week I visited Grandma Sarah. She has six cats and a very smart dog named Freckles," said Elly.

"Cats are okay, but I like dogs," replied Curt.

Elly asked, "Would you like to go with me to see Grandma Sarah tomorrow? Then you could see her dog Freckles."

"Okay, I'll go see Freckles. Grandma tells good stories and bakes great treats, too," answered Curt.

Grandma Sarah and some cats came to greet Elly and Curt when they arrived.

"Where is Freckles?" asked Curt.

"He's in the backyard playing with some of the other dogs," Grandma Sarah said with a smile.

"OTHER DOGS!" Both
Curt and Elly spoke at
once. Turning quickly,
they ran to the back yard.

"You were so busy looking
for cats the last time you
were here, you didn't see
the other dogs," laughed
Grandma Sarah.

"How many dogs do you have?" asked Curt. "Do you have names for all of them? Are they all the same kind of dog?"

"I have a dozen dogs," replied Grandma Sarah, "They all have names. Most are cocker spaniels like Freckles, but there are other kinds, too. These dogs can do lots of special things."

"A dozen dogs … that's twelve dogs," Curt said with amazement, "They may be able to do many things, but my dog can do anything!"

"A dozen dogs and six cats," added Elly.

Buster, the Hungarian vizsla
greeted them.

"When Curt's brother Grant was little,"
Grandma Sarah smiled, "Buster shared a
jar of face cream and a shower with him."

"My dog Wookie can do that, but it would take a hundred jars of face cream to cover him," laughed Curt.

"I see four cocker spaniels, but I don't see Freckles yet,"sighed Elly.

"Elmer, one of the cocker spaniels, loves cats," says Grandma.

"Julie, the collie is over there with your cousins Madeleine and Michaela. She loves children."

"My dog can do that. He loves
everybody," said Curt.

"Bozo, the English sheepdog, is a hero," said Grandma Sarah. "One day Julie fell into the river, and Bozo ran home to get help. He saved his dog friend."

"My dog can do that. St. Bernards save
skiers trapped in snow. I know Wookie
could do that and be a hero, too," said Curt.

Grandma Sarah said, "Listen, I hear some barking over by that big bush. Let's go see what is happening."

Lady and Lassie, two more cocker spaniels, had found the neighbor's pet raccoon.

"With so many younger dogs here, I am amazed that my two oldest dogs who can't see or hear very well are the ones who found him."

"Dog detective! My dog can do that.
Wookie has a really big nose. I
bet he could have sniffed out that
raccoon," boasted Curt.

As Elly scanned the yard some more, she was about to ask, "Where's Freckles?" when she saw another dog.

"Look over there," Elly pointed with delight.

"That's Doubtful, she's not any special kind of dog. Doubtful is my little clown, doing a special dance for you. She can do many tricks... for treats," Grandma added.

"Oh, doesn't that dog have the funniest smile?" Elly asked with a grin.

"That's Queenie, Doubtful's mother," answered Grandma Sarah. "She is smiling at her delightful dancing daughter."

"My dog is a clown, too. He ate his big piece of birthday cake in one giant bite without knocking his tiny hat from his head. He can do tricks, too, but he may not be as good a dancer as Doubtful," admitted Curt.

Grandma Sarah just smiled.

"Here comes Memphis the mutt, who loves to play fetch. Your arm will get tired before he is ready to quit playing," Grandma Sarah remarked as Curt tossed the ball.

"Wookie could fetch, too, if he wanted, but he probably would bury the ball in the yard. I don't know if he's hiding it or just wants to save it to play with it later," added Curt.

"Where's Freckles?" Elly asked again.

As they walked toward the house, Curt grinned and said, "I smell cookies."

"Oh no! Look at Katie the German shorthair, and Cookie, another cocker," exclaimed Grandma Sarah.

"They must love Grandma Sarah's cookies as much as we do," said Curt with surprise.

"It's a good thing there are more cookies in the oven," remarked Grandma Sarah as she lead the naughty dogs outside.

Curt said, "My dog did something like that once. When my family came home, Wookie was nosing through the garbage. He usually is such a good dog. But just like Cookie, he had a naughty helper, too. Merry, our golden retriever, was sitting in a corner like she had done nothing, but she had a noodle on her head."

Elly and Grandma Sarah had a good laugh about the story.

Elly said, "We haven't found Freckles yet."

Grandma thought for a moment, "I think I know where she is."

Elly and Curt followed Grandma.When she opened the bathroom door, there sat Freckles in a bathtub full of water!

Grandma giggled, "I keep forgetting how much that dog loves water."

Curt laughed and said, "I'm not sure Wookie would do that, but he probably needs a bath."

As they finished their cookies, Grandma told Curt and Elly, "Next time you visit the cats and the dogs, you must see the other animals who live here, too."

?!?

OTHER
ANIMALS?

?!?

THE END

CPSIA information can be obtained
at www.ICGtesting.com
Printed in the USA
BVHW020159211019
561581BV00013B/16/P